W9-AAC-919

A VERY SPECIAL CHRISTMAS TREE

BY HILARY LAZELL
ILLUSTRATED BY STEPHANIE RYDER

Brimax . Newmarket . England

It was Christmas Eve and Tinker the Squirrel was tucked up warm and snug in his little home in the big oak tree. He was staring at one of the pictures in his book. "Oh dear," he sighed as he shut the book.

Just then Mrs Rabbit was hopping by and heard Tinker sigh. Mrs Rabbit liked Tinker and knew how cheerful he usually was. It was very unlike him to sigh.

"What is the matter, Tinker?"
she called softly.
Tinker looked out of his hole.
"I have just seen the most
beautiful Christmas tree in my
book. It was covered with
shiny balls and pretty lights
that twinkled like stars."

Tinker showed Mrs Rabbit the picture in his book.
"It is beautiful," said Mrs Rabbit.
"I wish I had a tree like that instead of my dull brown one," said Tinker.

"Never mind Tinker," said Mrs Rabbit. "It will soon be Spring again and your tree will be covered in beautiful green leaves."

"Yes, you are right," said Tinker. "But I still wish it was prettier for Christmas."

"You should go to sleep now," said Mrs Rabbit. "Tomorrow is Christmas Day."
Mrs Rabbit hopped away. She did not like to see her friend so upset at Christmas time. She wondered if there was anything she could do to help.

On her way home she met
Herbert Hare, Freddie
Fieldmouse and Daisy Dormouse.
She told them all about the
tree in Tinker's book and how
unhappy Tinker was that his
tree was all bare.

"He is such a good little squirrel," said Mrs Rabbit. "It would be lovely if we could make his Christmas rather special."

"But how?" Freddie and Herbert said together.

"I have an idea," said Mrs Rabbit. "Come with me."

The next morning was Christmas
Day and Tinker was awakened by
a great deal of whispering. He
crept out of his hole to see
what all the noise was about.
All his friends were gathered
around the foot of the tree.

"Happy Christmas, Tinker," they all cried.
Tinker looked all around him and could hardly believe his eyes. While he had been asleep, his friends had been very busy.

They had been collecting pine cones, berries, nuts, mistletoe and holly, while some spiders had been spinning some delicate webs. When everything had been gathered together the animals started to decorate the tree.

All the gifts were hung from
the branches and the tree no
longer looked dull and bare.
As the snow began to fall the
tree sparkled brightly.

"It is beautiful," said Tinker. "Much more beautiful than the tree in my book. Thank you all so much. This is the best Christmas present I have ever had."

Say these words again.

tucked   snug
staring   sigh
matter   shiny
instead   leaves
hopped   friend
unhappy   lovely
gathered   believe